Zuba and the Crystal

Gem N Me
Penny Publishing Co.
United Black Fund

©All rights reserved. No part of this book may be reproduced in any manner what so ever with out written permission.

Dedication:
This book is dedicated to my mom, who always tells me it takes a village to raise a child and I would like to thank Ms. Penny and Ms. Kris for being apart of our village.

Ilustrator: Meetaashay

Once long ago in the galaxy of Crystal Utopia there lived a teenage girl. She wasn't just an ordinary teenage girl; she was a Princess, a different type of Princess. She was an alien princess named Zuba. Besides that, she was like any other 13-year-old teenager and wanted to try different things.

One day Zuba was on her phone scrolling on instagram, learning about human teenagers' lives. While she was scrolling, she saw a picture of a girl named Bri.

Zuba followed her instagram account. She noticed a crystal that was on Bri's necklace and was really interested in seeing what it was all about.

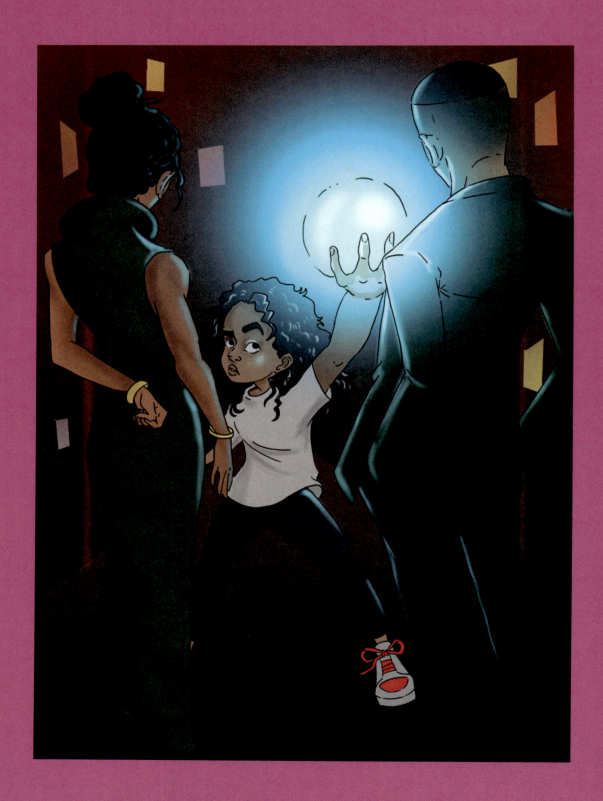

Zuba found her parents in the hall doing some royal business. She was curious about showing them the crystal she found. She needed to know if they had seen it before.

"Yes, Hunny, we have seen that crystal before," said mom.

Her parents said that the crystal was the last piece of the destructive crystal known to Utopia, and it was very valuable. "Zuba Hunny, that crystal is very dangerous," said her father.

That crystal has been used on earth by the Ion twins, Zion and Dion ,for evil doings.

Zuba's dad said, "let's send out the guards; there is another piece of the crystal still missing."

Zuba was now furious. She knew her parents wouldn't let her go to earth to find the missing piece of crystal even though she knew a lot about humans.

Her parents said humans did not know much about aliens, and if she turned into a human form, she might get caught because she was just a child.

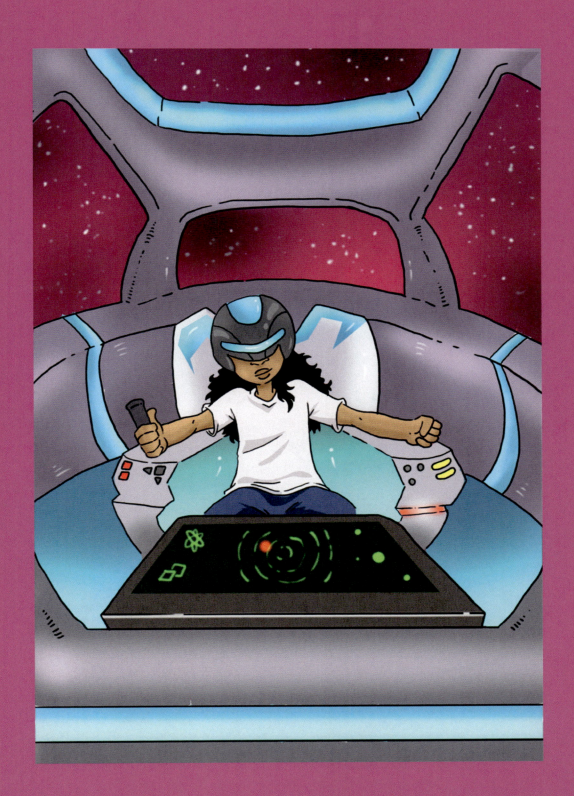

Zuba packed her things and took her private space pod to earth without her parents knowing, so she could go and find the crystal piece.

Zuba landed in Los Angeles, California. Since humans did not really know about aliens, Zuba had to turn into a human form. Zuba had an Instagram account under the name of Zoe. It was easy for her to switch names and go to school.

Zoe attended Los Angeles Middle School, where she met a girl named Bri. Zoe had been seeking out Bri and noticed the crystal necklace she was wearing on Instagram.

Zoe got into some of the same classes as Bri, and they quickly became best friends. Zoe and Bri did everything together, and you could never separate them. Zoe was a part of their family, and she liked being a part of a human family.

She said her parents got in a very tragic car accident. Bri's parents allowed Zoe to live with them temporarily.

During Zoe's time on Earth, Zoe started to realize that humans and aliens are just alike.

Zoe was ready to take her plan into action. She knew her ultimate mission was to get that crystal from Bri.

Instead of taking the necklace from her, she told Bri everything, even her alien secrets. Bri started laughing so hard and said, "good one Zoe."

Zoe tried to tell her, but she thought that she would believe her sometime soon.

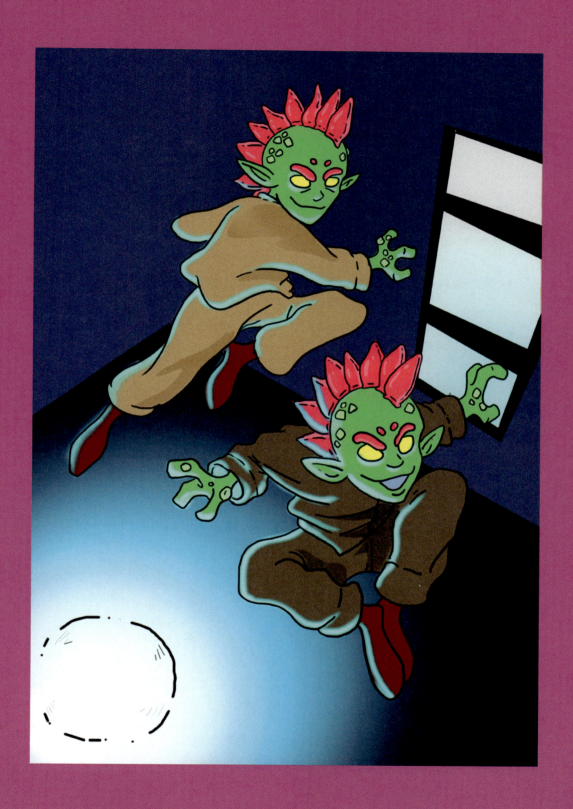

While Zoe confessed, the Ion twins overheard Zoe talking about the crystal through sounds waves that picked up from the galaxy. They had been onto Zoe the entire time she had been in Los Angeles.

The twins tried to take control of Zuba's parents' bodies but were unsuccessful. The Ion Twins stole a private spaceship jet to earth. The evil twins saw Zoe and immediately tried to take the crystal. Zoe asked what they were doing there, and they said, "to take the crystal and take you to our home."

Zoe asks Bri to give her the crystal for the second time before the Ion twins get a hold of it. Bri sees what's going on; she trusts Zoe and gives her the last piece of the crystal.

Then Zoe used her powers to take down the evil twins and stop them from destroying the earth. Then blasted the twins into a black hole so they could never return.

Zoe and Bri are still friends even though Zoe is an alien named Zuba. Humans are now allowed to go to the planet because she felt that humans were good.

Zuba's parents gave her a ceremony, which declared her head protector and she protected the galaxy of Crystal Utopia. Even though she was in a higher class, she still helped other people and treated everyone equally. Zuba thought Bri was the rightful person to keep the crystal safe.

The end!